6 7 8 9 10
❖
First Edition

RAINBOW FISH
TATTLE TALE

Text by Sonia Sander

Illustrations by Benrei Huang

■ HarperFestival®
A Division of HarperCollins*Publishers*

Rosie and Dyna were happy.

They were going to work together

on a science project.

"We will have the best project

in class," said Dyna.

"I know lots about growing algae."

Everything went well.

But Rosie and Dyna didn't always agree
on how to work together.

"Knock, knock," joked Rosie.

"Who is there?" asked Dyna.

"Sea," answered Rosie.

"Sea who?" asked Dyna.

"See that—we are almost done,"

said Rosie.

Dyna didn't think that was funny.

"We are *not* almost done.

We have not finished all of the

steps yet," said Dyna.

"We don't have to follow all of the
directions," said Rosie.

"I want to do it right," said Dyna.

11

Just then Miss Cuttle called,
"Recess time!"
At the Shipwreck playground
all the fish talked about their
science projects.

"How is your algae project going?"
Rainbow Fish asked Dyna.

"We would be finished if Rosie did not
joke around so much," said Dyna.

Angel thought this was interesting news.

After recess Rosie played with their algae.

"Roses are red, violets are blue.

This brown algae is sticky like glue,"

sang Rosie.

Dyna was unhappy.

The algae was now brown.

It should have been green!

"Now we have to start over!"

After school Angel asked Rosie

how she liked working with Dyna.

"The project would be more fun if she
didn't worry so much," said Rosie.
"She always tells me to be more careful."

"Oh, dear," said Angel.

"It does not sound like their project

is going well at all."

18

Angel swam over to Rusty and said,

"I heard that Dyna is being bossy and

Rosie is acting like a clown!"

19

Rusty swam over to Spike and said,

"Rosie and Dyna aren't getting along."

"Rosie is a good partner," said Spike.

"I always have fun working with her."

"It's fun until Miss Cuttle asks to
see your work," said Rusty.
"You get in trouble if it's not
done."

Rusty liked working with Dyna.

"I would work with Dyna any time,"
said Rusty. "She's so careful."

"You mean *boring*," said Spike.
"Dyna wants to do all the work
herself."

Dyna and Rosie had heard every word.

Their feelings were hurt.

"I thought you were my friend," said Dyna.

"How could you say that I am bossy?"

Rosie said, "I didn't say you were

bossy. Honest!"

"I thought working with you would
be fun," said Rosie.
"But if you think I'm a clown I don't
want to work with you at all."

"That is not what I said," Dyna replied.

"Ask Rainbow Fish. He was there!"

Rainbow Fish hated to see his
friends upset.
He thought he knew how this
problem started.
"The story got mixed up as it was
repeated," he said.

"You two could still be partners,"

said Rainbow Fish.

"Rosie, you always have fun ideas.

Dyna, you can make anything work.

I bet if you tried again, you could

have the best science project."

So Rosie and Dyna made up

and tried to work together.

Rosie told Dyna all about her ideas.

Dyna told Rosie what algae needs to grow.

Together they figured out how

to complete their science project.

This time the algae did grow.

It grew into a beautiful castle.

Their project was a success.